Up, Up
Down

by Kate Scott
Illustrated by Bill Ledger

Houghton Mifflin Harcourt.

In this story ...

Ann

Ann is strong. She has the power to lift rocks.

Jin

Mr. Trainer
(teacher)

Slink

2

Ann and her class were training near
the oak tree.

Jin shot up. He did some tricks and twists in the air.

Next, it was Ann's turn.
She flung the ball too hard.

The ball hit a wall.

Then it hit the tree.

"The branch will come down!"
Mr. Trainer said. "It will hit Slink!"

I will stop it!

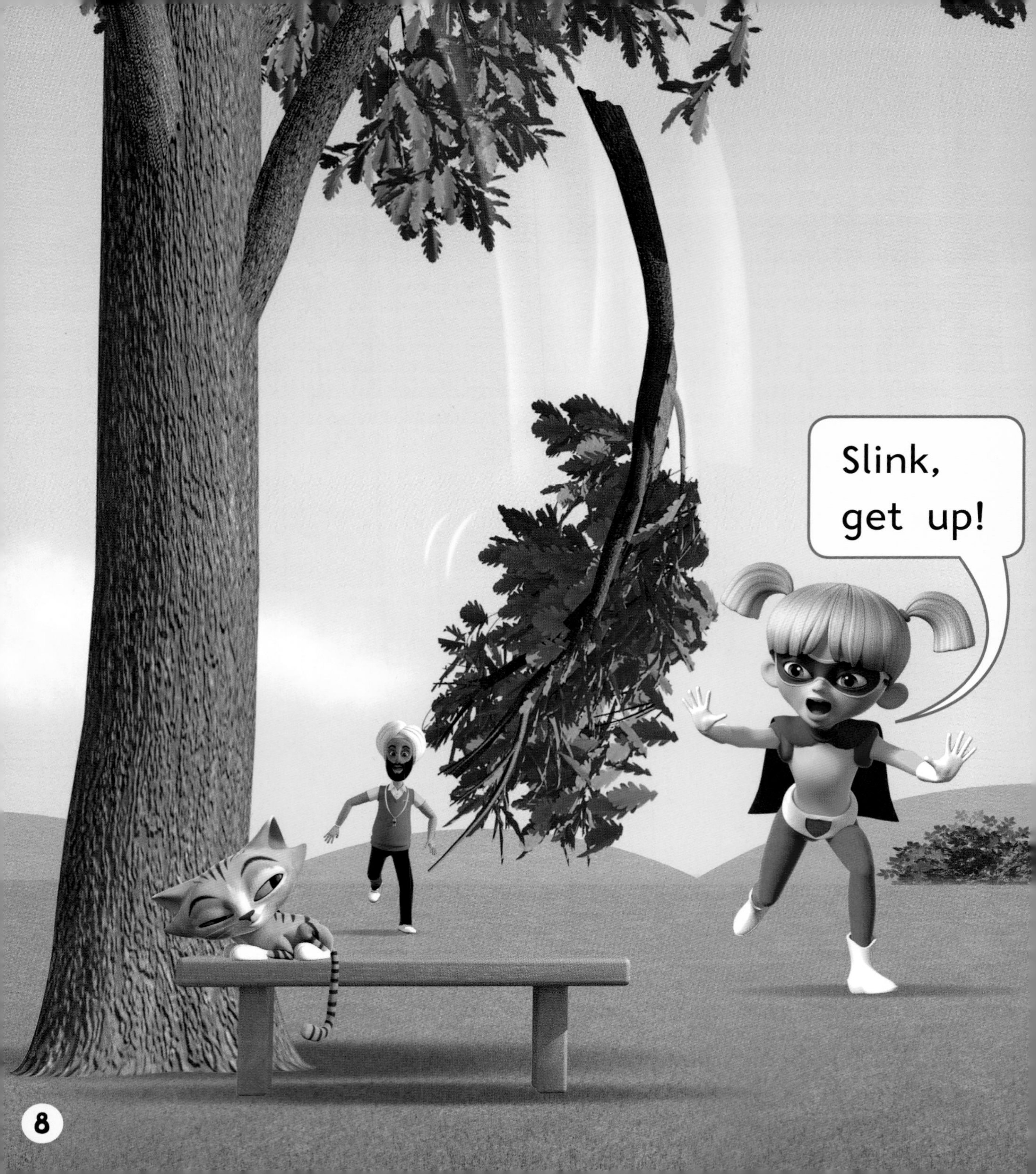
Slink, get up!

Ann did not stop the branch. It fell on the end of the bench.

Slink shot up into the air.
"Quick, Jin! Grab Slink!" said Mr. Trainer.

Jin did grab Slink, but he went too fast.

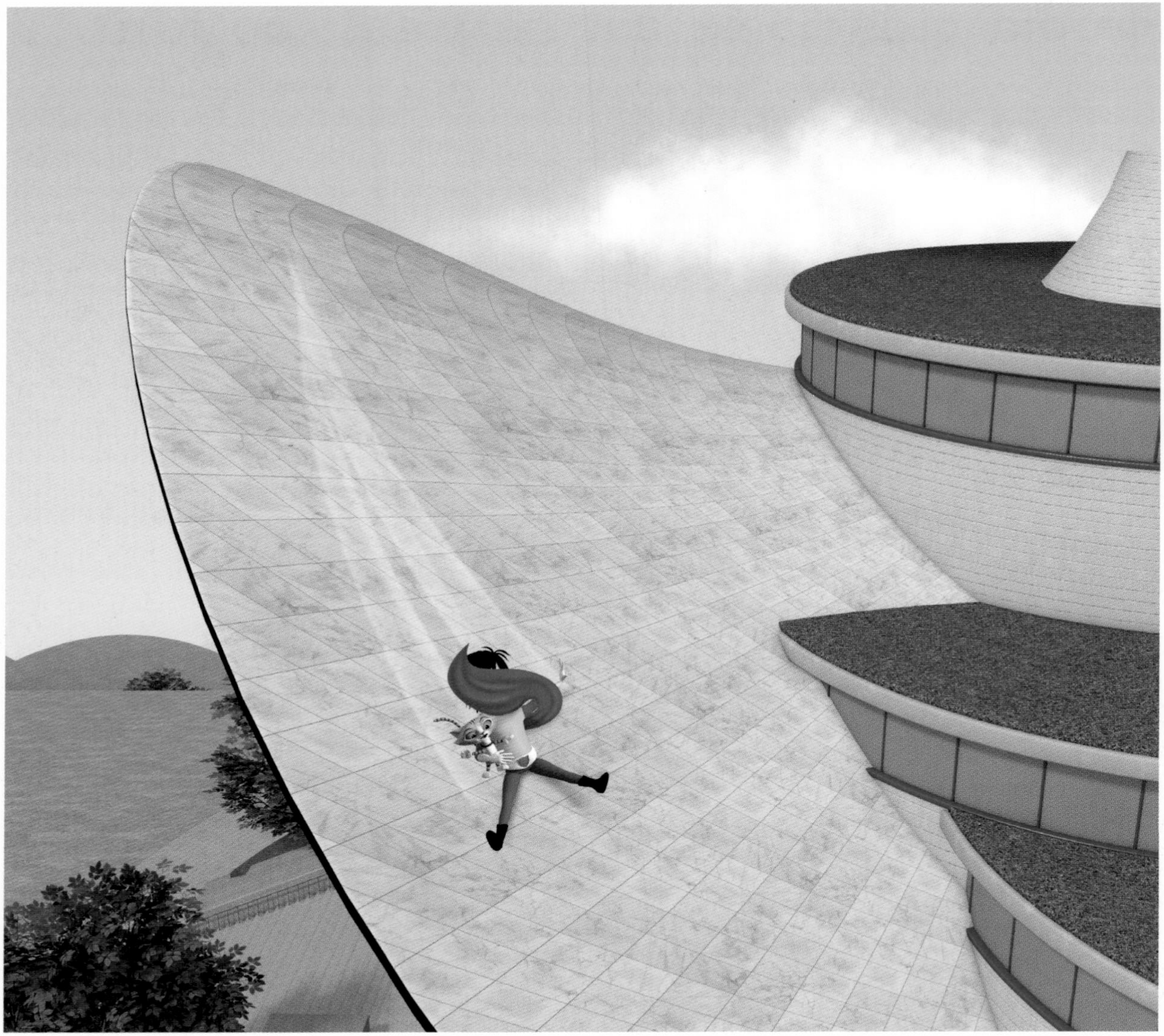

Jin and Slink hit the roof with a bump.
They skidded down.
"We cannot stop!" Jin said.

"They are going to fall from the roof!"
said Mr. Trainer.
"I will help," said Ann. "I have a plan."

Ann got Jin and Slink.

She put them down.

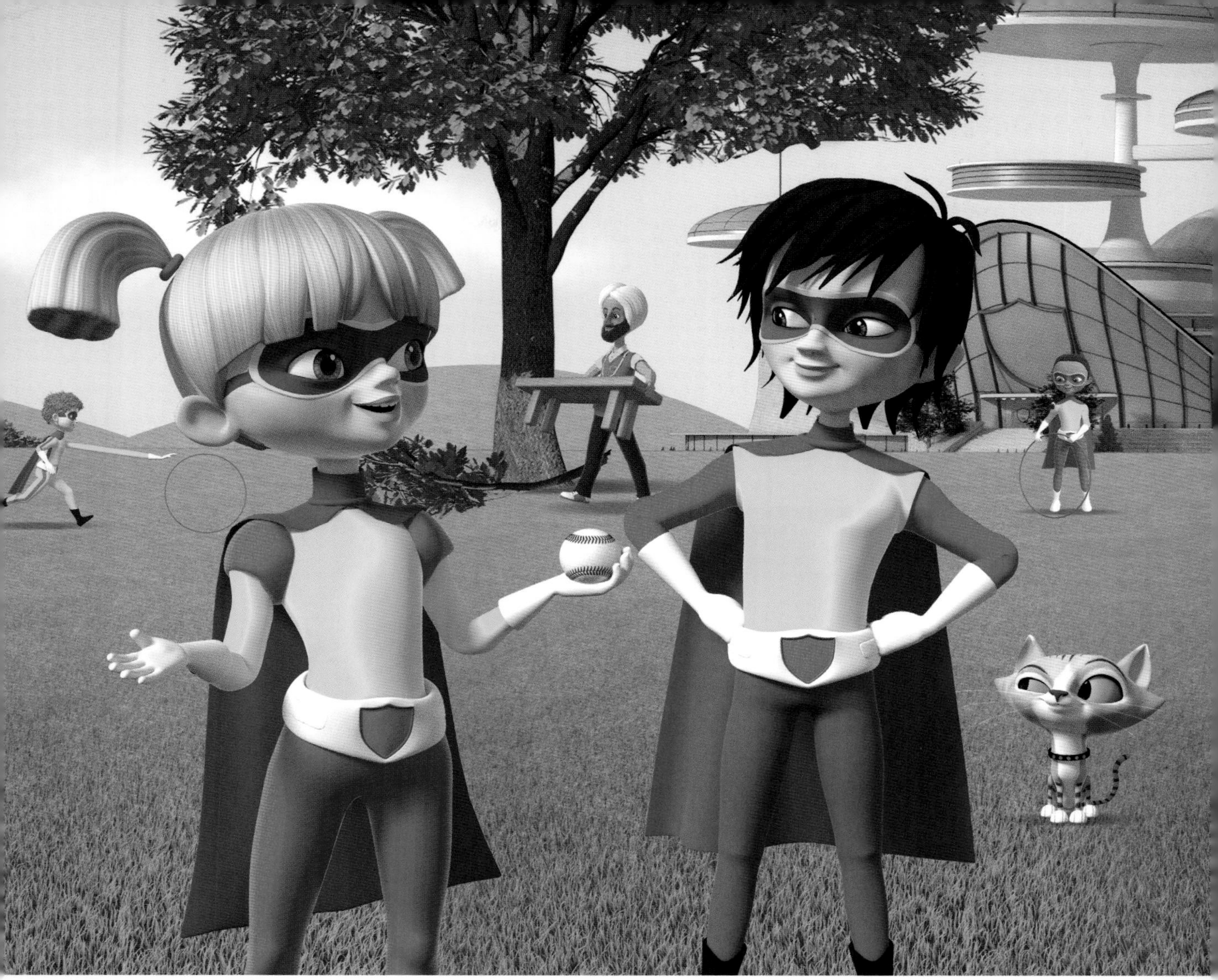

"I am glad you were there," Jin said.
"I did not like that."
"I will not throw the ball so hard again,"
Ann said.

Retell the story ....

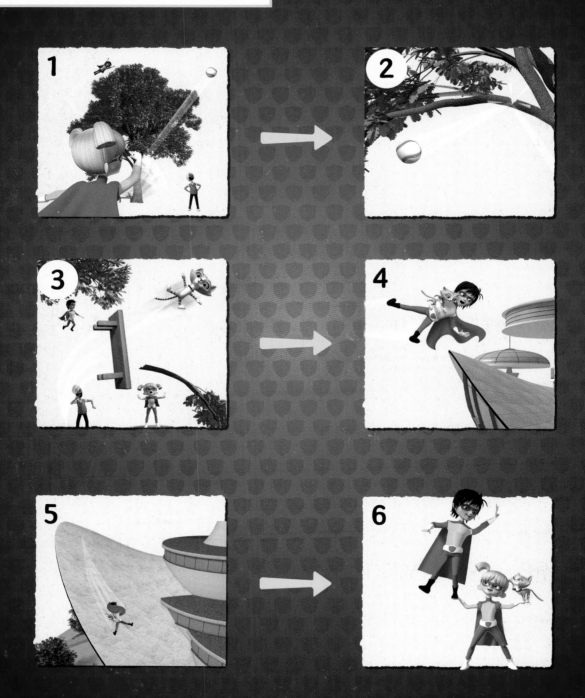